BOOKS BY LA

The Lost Kingdom

Holiday Romance

A Halloween Romance: Enchanted in Shadowbrook

A HALLOWEEN ROMANCE: ENCHANTED IN SHADOWBROOK

LAURA (L.A.) MARIANI

Ebook ISBN: 978-1-915501-71-4

1

EMILY

The heavy bell of Hartford's Books clanged with a deafening echo as I stepped inside, the golden morning light streaming through the front windows.

My fingers brushed along the spines of books, each telling its unique story, as I made my way to the counter and felt that familiar flutter in my chest. I loved being enveloped by these tales, knowing I could dive into any of them and be lost entirely.

I straightened the new release display and took a deep breath, letting the excitement sink in. What would today bring?

The clock struck nine, and I was ready for whatever awaited me.

. . .

Mrs Abernathy tottered in, and I handed over the cozy mystery she was waiting for. I joked that it reminded me of her, and she giggled. I prepared for the evening as she settled into an armchair to read.

Hours flew by helping customers choose books and ringing up sales. Though my days were full, my nights were empty. With a wistful sigh, I returned to the tasks - these books needed me, which was enough for now.

The bell above the door jingled cheerfully, yanking me from my thoughts. I saw a familiar figure breezing in, all sunshine and warmth, Abigail breezing in, blonde curls bouncing.

"Abigail!" my face lighting up. "You're a sight for sore eyes."

"Oh shush, you charmer." She waved her hand, her eyes sparkling. "I brought sustenance."

She hefted a large picnic basket onto the counter with a thud. The scent of fresh bread and cinnamon wafted up. My stomach rumbled traitorously.

"Have I told you lately that you're my favorite person?" I said, peering under the checkered cloth.

. . .

"Only every time I bring baked goods," she chuckled.

I poured two mugs, steaming and fragrant with hazelnut coffee; their warmth seeped into my hands as I carried them over to the seating area by the window. We settled with our feast spread before us. The world slowed to an easy beat as we chitchatted and nibbled.

Abigail bent forward eagerly, eyes twinkling with mischief. "You'll never guess who I saw at the market this morning."

I raised an eyebrow, fascinated. Our small town was always awash with gossip.

"Come on, take a guess!" Abigail urged.

"I don't know...the mayor?"

Abigail shook her head, grin broadening. "Nope! Try again."

"Old Man Jenkins?"

At that, Abigail exploded into a laughter. "Oh, Emily, your guesses are terrible! No, it was..." She paused for dramatic effect.

· · ·

I made a noncommittal noise, still lost in thought. My skin prickled with a weird awareness like I was on the verge of something big. Change loomed in the air.

"The mysterious stranger of Shadowbrook has returned. We had our first sighting today".

Shadowbrook was steeped in legends and mysteries that had captured my imagination since childhood. This place held secrets.

"Be serious, Abigail!"

"I am. It's October, the month when shadows wander Shadowbrook. Uuuuuh ..."

Abigail rambled on about the other gossip she'd gathered that morning. I tried to focus on her words, but my mind kept reverting to Shadowbrook 's legend.

The bookstore enveloped me in its familiar embrace, chasing away the chill. The worn oak shelves stood sentinel, their leather-bound treasures offering comfort and escape. An old book on ancient runes woven into red cloth covers sat on a shelf behind me; some said such symbols warded away evil or were used as portals to other worlds.

. . .

My mind began to wander. I yearned for that sense of freedom, that taste of something more. In my cozy haven, each day blended into the next in a comforting routine. But sometimes, late at night, I'd gaze out my window at the velvet sky and imagine. What if...

A flush rose on my cheeks. I'd been having those dreams again, hazy figures entwined in passion. I'd wake with my body aching, devoured by a desire I couldn't name. During the day, I could push it aside and lose myself in my books and work. But my nights were alight with nameless need.

I shifted in my chair; my skin felt too tight, my breath coming faster. I shouldn't be having such thoughts in the middle of the day, with my best friend sitting a few feet away.

Get a grip, Emily. You're being ridiculous. I lifted my coffee with a shaky hand and took a sip. The bitterness grounded me, bringing me back to the present.

But something was coming. I could feel it in my bones.

I shook my head, amused at my own foolish notions. The shop bell rang and I looked up. A handsome stranger stood in the doorway, looking brooding and intense. Our eyes locked, and the air crackled between us. Lips curving in a slow smile, he strode towards me.

· · ·

I couldn't ignore the quickening of my pulse and the shivery feeling that danced across my skin.

Abigail gasped, "It's him", she said.

2

DANIEL

The wind lashed through the streets of Shadowbrook, shifting the fallen leaves into a spirited dance. Chimes echoed from the bell tower of St. John's Church like a siren's call, beckoning me to my destiny.

I wandered toward the bookstore window, where I saw her.

A vision of astonishing beauty was framed against the glass: a flame-haired woman with eyes of liquid gold that pierced my soul and set my body on fire. Chestnut curls cascaded over delicate shoulders, her pale skin glowing in the autumn light.

My heart pounded as I stared in awe at this gorgeous creature. I wanted to know her and fill the ache in my chest and groin with her presence. I tried to remove my gaze from her; I was here now for a reason. I had to focus, but I was helpless against the lure of her presence.

. . .

Taking a deep breath, I stepped in the bookshop. The sweet aroma of cinnamon and fresh bread filled my lungs as I opened the door.

That's when I heard it. Her voice.

"Oh, Abigail, I just don't know anymore," she sighed. " I feel like I'm just going through the motions each day."

My ears perked up.

"Nonsense, Emily," came her friend's reply. "You can't give up hope. Your heart still has so much love left to give."

Emily. Her name was like music on my lips.

She didn't respond right away. "It's just ... I want more, you know?" she finally said. "Adventure, romance, magic. My life is so predictable."

Abigail chuckled. "Maybe you'll find it at the Halloween ball tonight."

"Do you really believe that?" Emily asked, a spark of curiosity in her voice.

. . .

"My dear, legends exist for a reason. You just have to open yourself to the mystery."

She turned as I closed the door, and our gazes locked for what felt like an eternity. In her hazel depths, I saw a fire raging beneath the surface, drawing me to her like a moth to a flame.

The moment our eyes connected, it was a spark that crackled in the air, a silent promise of something more. My mind spun at the intensity of our connection, and I knew I would never forget her.

I had to see her again. Tonight. Under the harvest moon, with magic crackling in the air.

"Welcome to Hartford's Books," she said with a shiver.

"It's him," her friend whispered.

"Can I help you find anything?" Emily continued.

"I couldn't help overhearing your conversation earlier," I began, moving closer to her. "About the legends surrounding this town--it drew me here."

. . .

Her cheeks reddened, but she held my gaze. "Oh, you heard that?"

"Are you new in town? What brings you to Shadowbrook?" changing the subject.

"Yes - Daniel, Daniel Foster." I extended my hand, desperate to touch her skin. A lightning bolt rushed inside me as our fingers touched.

Our eyes locked briefly before Emily cleared her throat shyly and turned away.

"Just passing through," I said, my voice low and secretive. Emily's eyes widened as she took me in, her cheeks tinged with a deep blush.

"But this place intrigues me. As do you, Emily."

Her gaze dropped to the ground, but I could still see a trace of excitement on her face. "I'm not that interesting," she mumbled.

I chuckled and stepped until I could feel the softness of my breath against her skin. "I disagree," I said softly. My heart was beating fast.

Emily raised her eyes to mine. My heart raced faster than any train on a track, and my cock was hard.

. . .

"Meet me tonight at the Halloween ball," I murmured. "Let's see what wild magic we can conjure under the harvest moon."

She hesitated before agreeing, but it felt like an ancient prophecy coming true right before our eyes when she finally did. The autumn air seemed to crackle with electricity as I left the bookshop, ready for whatever destiny lay ahead.

3

DANIEL

The grand doorway of the ballroom opened, and Emily emerged, an ethereal vision in her vintage emerald dress. The fabric adhered to her curves like a second skin. Her chestnut hair was swept up, only a few tendrils framing her face. Behind an ornate mask, her hazel eyes flashed with excitement.

She almost seemed too perfect to be of this world; she looked like a character from one of the worn novels she loved, brought to life right before me.

My heart raced, yearning to go to her and take her in my arms. And then she looked at me and smiled.

"Daniel," she said softly and held out her hand.

• • •

My skin tingled at the electric touch of hers. With our hands clasped, I guided her onto the dance floor as the music streamed around us. I slid my free hand around her waist, pulling her close until our bodies were pressed against each other's. I am sure she could fill my hardened cock pushing against her dress, but I didn't care.

"You look beautiful tonight," I muttered, drinking at the sight of her. A blush stained her cheeks. She stared up at me through her lashes.

We danced in a deep silence that seemed to engulf us as if the rest of the room didn't exist. My heart thundered against my chest, and I wondered if she could feel it. Her lips were slightly parted, and I leaned closer, my whole body pulled inexorably towards her like a moth to flame.

Our noses brushed, and Emily's eyelids fluttered closed in anticipation...

before she unexpectedly stepped back from me, her hand though still firmly clutched in mine.

"Daniel, I..." She stuttered, a furrow forming between her perfect brows.

I froze, cursing myself for moving too fast. "Forgive me. I shouldn't have assumed…"

. . .

"No," she said quickly, her voice barely more than a whisper. Emily glanced around the crowded ballroom, couples twirling past us in an endless vortex of color and light. I came closer still, my breath warm against her ear.

"Perhaps we could continue this conversation somewhere more private?"

Desire roared through me, louder than the music and more powerful than a storm.

Every second felt precious now. I have to have her.

She nodded hesitantly and followed me away from the dance floor, weaving through the partygoers until we slipped out onto a secluded area outside the French windows. The night air was cool against my heated skin, and Emily hugged herself against the chill.

I moved behind her and rested my hands on her hips, feeling the rhythm of her breathing beneath them; she leaned back against me with a faint sigh. I could see her soft breasts rising beneath the green fabric.

"Emily..." I turned her in my arms to see her face. Her creamy skin was glowing.

· · ·

"I know we haven't known each other long, but I feel like I've been searching for you my whole life. I want you, baby."

Emily traced her fingers along my jawline before settling them on either side of my neck. "I feel the same," she whispered into my ear. "Like I was always destined to find you here in Shadowbrook."

I grabbed her face in my hands, my fingertips digging into her skin as I tilted her head back. Our lips met with a force that stole the air, and she gasped in pleasure. My tongue explored every inch of her mouth. Emily clung to me, her fingers threading through my hair. I pulled her closer and closer until our breaths mingled.

Breaking apart for only a moment, I looked at her, feeling a swell of emotion so strong it threatened to break me in two. I knew no matter what happened, I would always return for her.

The touch of Emily's skin against mine was like a bolt of electricity that sent my body into overdrive. My hunger for her became unbearable as she worked on the buttons of my shirt, her fingers grazing my bare chest and awakening every nerve ending. My skin burned hotter with the knowledge that I was hers alone, and I pulled her closer, desperate to taste more of her.

· · ·

She moaned in response as I trailed my lips down her neck, feeling a thrill as she grabbed onto me and dug her nails deep into my back. She bit down on her lip, sending me to the edge, and I claimed her mouth again. Emily responded to each movement of my lips with ferocity, dragging her nails along my spine and making me shudder with pleasure. With one final thrust, I backed her up against a tree and pinned her there, desperate to feel more of her.

My hands shook as I hastily removed her clothes, baring her beautiful curves and delicate lace lingerie.

I took a moment to devour every inch of her with my eyes, wanting to etch this moment of perfect beauty into my memory forever.

"Make love to me, Daniel," she whispered.

"No. Tonight, I want to fuck you hard so you will never forget me".

I lifted her up, and she wrapped her legs around my waist. Laying her down in the soft grass, I worshipped every inch of her with my hands and mouth.

I wanted her so badly. My hands scrolled across her skin and moved hungrily across her body, and I yanked her panties down with a single tug, eager to see all of her.

· · ·

"Emily," I breathed, "You look incredible."

"Fuck me," she begged in a throaty voice that set my blood on fire.

I had already waited too long - I needed to be inside her. My aroused body shuddered as I stood naked before her, my manhood thick with need. With an animalistic growl, I sunk into her welcoming depths.

Emily wrapped her legs around my waist and dug her heels into my back, crying out with pleasure as I pushed deeper and deeper into her embrace. Our bodies moved together as we found our rhythm, my thrusts growing more passionate and desperate until the flood was coming, and there was no longer a way to hold back.

"Are you close, baby?" I asked, needing the sensation of being together even more.

"Yes, yes!" came her reply.

I squeezed my eyes shut, biting my lip against the overwhelming bliss courting throughout every limb as I reached my peak. At that moment, I knew that Emily would be mine forever.

4

EMILY

I woke up, my pussy sore from a night of passionate lovemaking. I had never experienced anything like it. But Abigail's words still rang in my ear, "It's him," she said.

Can he be the mysterious stranger that haunts Shadowbrook every year in October?

"What's wrong?" Daniel asked, coming up behind me.

"Do you see that?" I said, too scared to ask.

A faint shimmer in the air, like heat rising off pavement. Except this was October in New England.

"It started a few days ago. It happens every October: streetlights flicker at odd hours. Mysterious clanking sounds echo from empty buildings. Howls and shrieks pierce the night, far too primal to be ordinary animals. Some in town blame pranksters, while others whisper about restless spirits. And then, magically, everything goes back to normal in November".

Daniel looked at me, pensous. He was holding back.

"Emily," he whispered, "We haven't got much time, baby. Let's make the most of it".

"What? Are you going somewhere? You have just arrived ... ".

"Take me with you," I blurted out, not knowing where that came from.

"I can't, baby. There is nothing I would want more, but I can't", Daniel pleaded.

"Why not? Everything you said to me last night was a lie ..." I screamed at him, furious.

"Baby, come here," he said, trying to get close to me.

"Don't touch me!" I shouted.

· · ·

"Baby, the only way for you to come with me is ..." , he paused "if you were dead!"

And then, something clicked. He IS the mysterious stranger that haunts our town.

An unnatural mist hung low, muting sounds. The wind picked up, blowing leaves in vortexes. An unearthly moan split the air.

"They are looking for me", he said.

5

EMILY

"We need to figure this out," I said determined to uncover the truth behind the hauntings plaguing our town and freeing Daniel from his curse.

Daniel's green eyes obscured by concern. "Emily, it's too dangerous."

"I'm not afraid," I shot back, adrenaline coursing.

"Are you sure about this?" he asked again. I lifted my chin. "I'm sure."

"Emily, this could be dangerous," Daniel repeated, his voice edged with concern.

. . .

I met his gaze. "I know, but it's the only way. Don't you see?"

We left the house, autumn leaves crunching under our feet as we walked briskly. I shivered from the chill or trepidation; I wasn't sure.

Daniel fell into step beside me, his hand brushing mine.

"We need to search the archives in the town hall basement," I said decisively. "There must be records of the original land deeds, maybe even journals from the founders."

Daniel raised an eyebrow. "And you think the sheriff will let us search down there?"

I smirked. "Sheriff Cooper owes me a favor or two. I'll get us in."

He giggled. "Why do I get the feeling you're trouble?"

"Maybe I am," I said lightly, my pulse quickening at the flirtatious banter.

Focus, I reminded myself.

· · ·

We arrived at the town hall, an imposing brick building. Sheriff Cooper met us at the door, keys in hand.

"Emily Hartford, the things I do for you," he sighed, showing us inside.

The basement was musty, filled with endless shelves of boxes. We got to work searching, the air heavy with tension.

What were we looking for exactly? And what would we do if we found it? My breath caught as I uncovered an ancient leather journal.

I carefully opened it, the old pages crackling. The handwriting was faded but legible.

"Listen to this," I said. "'The shadows grow long in this valley. I fear we have disturbed things better left buried.'"

I looked up at Daniel.

"There's more," I went on. "'Strange events plague us. Livestock slaughtered, crops failing. The natives whisper of an ancient evil in these hills.'"

Daniel moved closer, reading over my shoulder. I was intensely aware of his nearness, my skin prickling. Focus, Emily.

. . .

I took a deep breath to steady my nerves. I exchanged a worried glance with Daniel. Sheriff Cooper spoke up.

"I think we need to notify my department, get some extra patrols around town until we figure this out," he said.

The musty scent of aging paper fills my nostrils as we pore over the historical society's archives. Frayed photographs, leather-bound journals, and moth-eaten newspapers litter the table before us. Daniel's brow is furrowed as he skims a crumbling book while Sheriff Cooper examines some old property records.

My eyes scan the faded words of a diary I discovered on a bottom shelf. The author vividly describes sinister rituals held deep in Shadowbrook's forest over a century ago. Disturbing accounts of torchlight processions, animal sacrifices, and chants uttered in a strange tongue.

A chill runs down my spine, and I suppress a shudder.

I feel Daniel's hand on my shoulder, his touch warm and reassuring. He gives me a slight nod, sensing my unease. My heart flutters despite the unsettling discoveries we've made.

I should be wary of getting too close. What if I lose him forever? But try as I might, I cannot resist the magnetic pull I feel toward him.

One look into Daniel's smoldering gaze banishes those doubts. I feel drawn into his world.

My heart leaps when I uncover an old article about a gruesome murder at the haunted house. The murder of Daniel Foster. His shoulder brushes mine, and I feel a delicious shiver.

"What have we gotten ourselves into?" Sheriff Cooper mutters, running a hand through his sandy brown hair in disbelief.

I glance over at him, seeing the concern etched on his face. He's always been protective of this town and its people. The thought of some unknown evil lurking close to home has shaken him.

Clearing my throat, I turned to the photographs, searching for clues. And there, a familiar sight appeared in a black-and-white image from the late 1800s.

"The abandoned Crawford mansion," I said. "It was one of the locations mentioned in those legends. That is where we need to go next".

———

The creaking door gave way under my trembling hand. I peered into the darkness of the abandoned mansion, its once grand foyer now covered in layers of dust and cobwebs. Shadows danced across the peeling wallpaper as Daniel and John's flashlight beams swept past me.

"This place gives me the creeps," John whispered, his voice echoing eerily through the empty halls.

I steeled my nerves as we stepped inside, each footstep announcing our presence.

Daniel's hand grazed my back reassuringly as he moved beside me. My skin tingled at his touch. Focus!

I swept my flashlight along the walls, illuminating strange symbols etched into the crumbling plaster. They seemed to squirm and twist as if alive—dark magic.

A heavy book lay open on a nearby table, its pages covered in illegible scrawl. I traced the cryptic letters, a chill running down my spine. It was the same old book with ancient runes woven into red cloth covers from my bookshop.

John's voice broke the silence. "Guys, look at this." He was examining a large symbol carved into the floorboards, his brow furrowed. Daniel and I joined him, the three of us transfixed.

The musty air grew heavier with each step, oppressive as if the mansion was watching us. I could sense a dark presence lurking, just out of sight. The shadows deepened, writhing at the edges of my vision. Get out, a voice whispered. Daniel.

I swallowed hard. "Do you guys hear that?"

Daniel's jaw was tense, his eyes alert. "We're not alone." His words sent a chill through me. "They are here to get me".

John let out a nervous laugh. "You're just trying to scare us." But the quiver in his voice gave him away. He felt it, too.

I swept my flashlight along the walls, searching for I knew not what. Anything to make sense of the dread welling up inside me.

Then I saw it. A figure, vaguely human-shaped, flickering at the end of the hallway. Beckoning.

I stumbled back with a gasp. Daniel's hand grasped my arm, steadying me. His touch grounded me and kept the terror at bay.

"Emily?" His eyes searched mine, filled with concern.

Before I could answer, a loud bang shattered the heavy silence. We whirled to see the double doors at the entrance slam shut. John leaped forward, grabbing the handle and pulling with all his might. It didn't budge.

"No, no, no, this can't be happening!" Panic laced John's voice.

We were trapped. And we were not alone. The presence surrounding us was no longer content to lurk unseen. It had awakened, and it had found its prey.

Us.

I shook my head, trying to clear the paralyzing fear threatening to overwhelm me. We had to keep moving.

"Come on," I said, grabbing Daniel's hand and pulling him down the hall, away from the apparition. John scrambled after us.

Our flashlights sliced through the oppressive darkness as we moved through room after room, finding only dust and cobwebs. No way out. The whispers returned, hissing words I couldn't quite make out.

John whirled around. "Did you hear that?"

"We can't stop," Daniel said firmly. "There has to be a way out of here somewhere." But I could hear the doubt creeping into his voice.

. . .

I swept my light over the faded wallpaper, looking for anything out of place: a hidden door, a loose board. As we reached the end of the hall, a section of the wallpaper caught my eye. It seemed ever so slightly warped.

I moved closer, heart racing. "Help me with this," I said, handing Daniel the flashlight. We clawed at the paper, peeling it back to reveal a narrow opening.

"A passageway," Daniel breathed.

John let out a shaky laugh. "Emily, you did it!"

Daniel ducked inside first, John and I close behind. The passage sloped downwards into the darkness. We didn't know where it led, but it was better than waiting to be slaughtered by vengeful ghosts.

Hand in hand, we descended into the shadows.

The passage leveled out, opening into a large chamber. Our lights danced over the walls, revealing faded frescoes and strange symbols. My skin prickled. This place felt ancient.

In the center sat a stone pedestal holding an ornate box. I moved closer, pulse racing. This had to be it—the artifact we were searching for.

. . .

Daniel tensed. "Careful, Emily."

I reached out slowly, hesitating, then lifted the lid. Inside lay an amulet on a golden chain. The stone glowed faintly blue in the flashlight beam.

"Is that..." John whispered.

"The amulet. It must be." I picked it up gently. A shockwave of energy jolted through me, and I gasped, nearly dropping it. The whispers around us grew louder, more frantic.

Daniel gripped my shoulders. "Are you alright?" His eyes were full of concern.

I took a shaky breath. "I think so. But this amulet...it's powerful. I can feel it."

John leaned in. "Those symbols match the ones upstairs. This has to be the key to stopping whatever's haunting this place."

I clasped the amulet tightly, feeling its energy thrumming through me. "I have been here a thousand of times, and I never saw it before", Daniel said pulling me close, his warmth steadying me.

· · ·

I looked into his eyes, my heart swelling.

"Let's end this," I said firmly. The amulet glowed brighter, responding to my resolve. I could feel its power awakening, ready to unleash.

The shadows swirled and gathered before us, morphing into grotesque shapes. A chorus of angry whispers surrounded us as the spirits closed in.

I gripped the amulet, willing its power forth. "Get back!' I shouted.

The spirits recoiled momentarily but then resumed their advance. One wraith-like form lunged toward me, its clawed hands outstretched.

I stumbled back with a scream, directly into the path of another specter. Daniel pulled me out of the way just in time, placing himself between me and the attacking spirits.

"Use the amulet, Emily!" he yelled over the rising din.

My hands shook as I raised the amulet again. I had to focus, to tap into its power. The spirits clawed at Daniel as he tried to fend them off. We were running out of time.

· · ·

I closed my eyes and channeled every ounce of energy and intent into the amulet. It began to glow hot in my hands. The angry whispers turned into shrieks of pain and fury.

I opened my eyes to see the spirits falling back, writhing as if burned by the amulet's light. But one persistent wraith continued to fight through, fixated on me with evil intent.

Before I could react, it dove forward, spectral hands outstretched for my throat. Daniel shouted my name and knocked me out of the way, taking the brunt of the attack himself.

He fell to his knees with a choked cry, clutching his chest as the spirit's touch burned through him.

"No!" I screamed. Rage and fear surged within me. The amulet flared brighter than ever in response.

I thrust the amulet toward the attacking spirit. Blinding light erupted, enveloping the shadowy form until it dissolved with an unearthly wail.

The remaining spirits shrieked and fled, retreating into the mansion's dark corners. An unnatural hush fell over the chamber.

I dropped the amulet, gripped his shoulders, and fell to Daniel's side. "Daniel! Are you alright?"

· · ·

He looked up, face pale but eyes clear. "I'll be okay. Had to protect you."

Tears spilled down my cheeks. I thought I'd lost him. But he was willing to sacrifice himself for me.

I threw my arms around him, "I thought I'd lost you," I whispered.

He held me close. "You won't lose me. No matter what. I will always come back to you."

I kissed him fiercely then, no longer afraid. Daniel returned my kiss with equal passion. He was mine, and I was his.

We broke apart, breathless. There was no time for more - the remaining spirits could return at any moment.

John helped Daniel to his feet.

"We end this tonight," I said.

John nodded. "What's the plan?"

I held up the amulet. Its light seemed to pulse with power. "We use this. All the clues we found here suggest it's a talisman of great power."

Daniel touched his chest where the spirit had struck him. "It's our best chance. But we have to lure the spirits to us."

"The ritual chamber," John said. "That's where we first stirred them up. If we perform the ritual again..."

"We can draw them out." I finished his thought. It was dangerous, but it could work.

Without another word, we began preparations. Thankfully John had brought holy water and we found ritual herbs to strengthen the amulet. Daniel created protective sigils and wards.

I clutched the amulet, focusing my energy on it. So much was at stake - our town, lives, and future together. Failure was not an option.

Too soon, we were ready. The air crackled with energy as we entered the ritual chamber. Shadows gathered, restless spirits waiting for us to make our move.

John, Daniel, and I stood together.

Hand in hand, we began the ritual that would end this nightmare. The spirits swirled around us, the battle for Shadowbrook had begun.

6

DANIEL

E mily began to perform the ritual clutching the amulet.

I squeeze her hand, bracing for the evil descending upon us. Emily leans into me; I will keep her safe. Tenderness sweeps over me as I meet her eyes, seeing my determination mirrored back at me.

I will not let them take me back into the shadows. I have too much to lose now.

The wind howls outside, banging the shutters violently. It is time. Shadowy figures approach; the battle has begun. Emily grasps my hand as we prepare for the fight ahead.

"Stay behind me," I murmur, pulling Emily close. The specters draw nearer, screaming and clawing at us. We fight back with iron rods and pokers from the fireplace, forcing them back into the night.

. . .

Gasping, Emily crumples against me. I brush a stray hair from her face, heart swelling. Hand in hand, we turn to face the terrors of the night once more. The ghouls resume their assault, and strike John.

"John", Emily screams.

I feel his pulse and throat, "He is alive", I said to reassure her.

Together, we use iron and holy water to force the specters back, holding the amulet. The overpowering chill lingers in the hall, and I pull Emily close, my concern growing. We may have turned back this wave, but the war still rages. She squeezes my hand.

A wispy figure emerges from the shadows, and I push Emily behind me. I slash at it with iron. Emily splashes it with holy water, repeating the magic words, and it dissolves into mist. Another shriek echoes —the remaining spirits are regrouping. We steel ourselves for the next onslaught.

Side by side, we stride toward the swelling darkness. Iron and holy water in hand, we prepare to face our destiny.

. . .

We burst into the hall, lashing out. Emily chants words of banishment, driving the spirits back until they dissipate.

Panting, Emily, and I survey the now-empty room.

But our moment of peace is shattered by an unearthly howl that rends the night air. Emily tenses in my arms, eyes widening.

"They're not finished with us yet," I say grimly, taking her hand. My protective instincts surge, along with another, more primal feeling. Even amidst the danger, Emily's touch ignites my desire.

Shadowy figures emerge from the mist, ghouls, and specters we thought banished. Their ghostly forms drift toward us, and spectral hands outstretched hungrily.

Emily's grip tightens on mine.

Emily and I battle the apparitions, our weapons-making short work of them. My gaze strays to her more often than it should, admiring her fierce beauty. "Whatever happens, I love you Daniel", she shouted, holding the amulet.

Suddenly, it bursts on fire. A growling desperate cry into the night follows. The doors unlock and light streams in. They are gone.

. . .

I hold her close.

She smiles up at me, eyes shining.

I gaze down at Emily, holding her close. Her cheeks are flushed from the battle, wisps of chestnut hair escaping her braid. She has never looked more beautiful.

"Emily..." I begin, then falter.

She places a finger over my lips. "I know," she says softly. "I've known for a while now."

My breath catches.

Emily continues, "I love you."

I cup her face tenderly. "And I love you, Emily, with all I am."

Our lips meet in a kiss that banishes any lingering chill from the night's battle. Emily melts against me with a happy sigh, her arms twining around my neck. We break apart slowly, foreheads touching, matching smiles on our faces.

. . .

The rising sun bathes us in golden light. A new day dawns on Shadowbrook, full of promise. Panting, hearts pounding from adrenaline, we look at each other - desire in our eyes.

EMILY

Daniel and I were finally alone, our bodies pressed against each other, lips locked in a fiery kiss.

"Emily," he murmured against my neck, sending shivers down my spine.

"Daniel," I moaned, running my hands through his hair.

His hands roamed over my body, igniting a fire I never knew existed.

"You are mine, forever," he said, pulling back slightly to look into my eyes.

I nodded, unable to form words as my desire for him grew stronger.

He picked me up effortlessly and carried me to the bed, laying me down gently before taking off his shirt. My eyes drank at his sculpted abs, muscles rippling with every movement.

"God, you're beautiful," he whispered, leaning down to capture my lips again.

Our bodies moved together in perfect harmony, sweat glistening on our skin as we explored each other's bodies with reckless abandon.

"Daniel," I gasped, feeling my release approaching.

"Let go, Emily," he encouraged, his fingers working their magic on my body.

As we climaxed together, I knew this was only the beginning of our love story.

"Stay with me," I whispered, snuggling into his arms.

"Always," he replied, holding me close as we drifted off to sleep, eager for the next chapters of our adventure together through eternity.

GET YOUR FREE EBOOK

Sign up the Laura (L.A.) Mariani mailing list for a FREE steamy romance.

You'll be the first to hear about new releases, exclusive offers, bonus content and all Laura's news. You can even email her back. She loves chatting with her readers!

To claim your free ebook visit:
https://laura-mariani-author.ck.page/freeshortstory

ABOUT THE AUTHOR

Laura Alexandra (L.A.) Mariani is a best selling author of Short & Steamy Romance ǀ Where Alpha Males Meet Fierce Heroines for Sweet Endings, your go-to author for captivating romance tales that will sweep you off your feet and keep you on the edge of your seat!

When Laura is not weaving stories of love, desire and suspense, you'll find her exploring the vibrant streets of London, drawing inspiration from its hidden corners and bustling markets, or strolling through the charming streets of Paris, savoring street food in Rome, or relaxing on a sun-kissed beach in Bali, her journeys fuelling her creativity and infuse her stories with wanderlust.

You can also follow her on

𝕏 x.com/PeopleAlchemist
instagram.com/lauramariani_author
facebook.com/lauramarianiauthor

Printed in Great Britain
by Amazon